P9-CRO-633

DISNEY

CLUB PENGUIN™

The Official Stage Playbook

By Katherine Noll

Grosset & Dunlap

GROSSET & DUNLAP
Published by the Penguin Group
Penguin Group (USA) Inc., 375 Hudson Street, New York, New York 10014, USA
Penguin Group (Canada), 90 Eglinton Avenue East, Suite 700,
Toronto, Ontario M4P 2Y3, Canada
(a division of Pearson Penguin Canada Inc.)
Penguin Books Ltd., 80 Strand, London WC2R ORL, England
Penguin Group Ireland, 25 St. Stephen's Green, Dublin 2, Ireland
(a division of Penguin Books Ltd.)
Penguin Group (Australia), 250 Camberwell Road,
Camberwell, Victoria 3124, Australia
(a division of Pearson Australia Group Pty. Ltd.)
Penguin Books India Pvt. Ltd., 11 Community Centre,
Panchsheel Park, New Delhi—110 017, India
Penguin Group (NZ), 67 Apollo Drive, Rosedale,
North Shore 0632, New Zealand (a division of Pearson New Zealand Ltd.)
Penguin Books (South Africa) (Pty.) Ltd., 24 Sturdee Avenue,
Rosebank, Johannesburg 2196, South Africa

Penguin Books Ltd., Registered Offices:
80 Strand, London WC2R ORL, England

The publisher does not have any control over and does not assume any
responsibility for author or third-party websites or their content.

The scanning, uploading, and distribution of this book
via the Internet or via any other means without the permission
of the publisher is illegal and punishable by law. Please purchase
only authorized electronic editions and do not participate in or
encourage electronic piracy of copyrighted materials.
Your support of the author's rights is appreciated.

© 2009 Disney. All rights reserved.
Used under license by Penguin Young Readers Group. Published by
Grosset & Dunlap, a division of Penguin Young Readers Group,
345 Hudson Street, New York, New York 10014. GROSSET & DUNLAP
is a trademark of Penguin Group (USA) Inc. Printed in the U.S.A.

Library of Congress Control Number: 2009016119

ISBN 978-0-448-45183-1   10 9 8 7 6 5 4 3 2 1

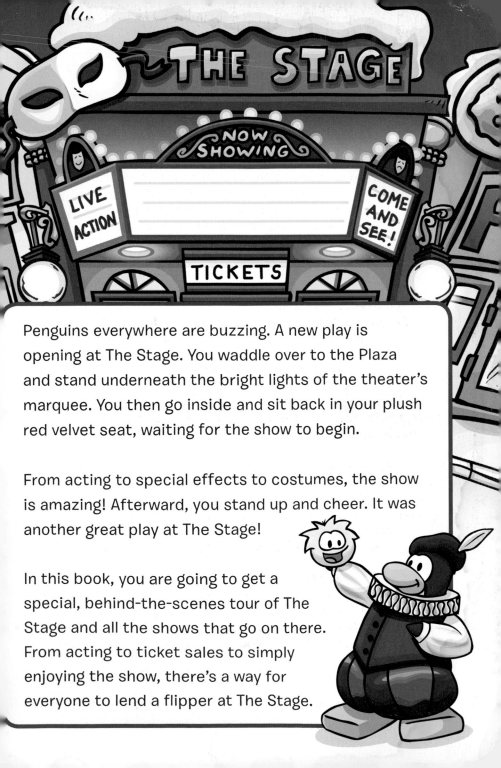

Penguins everywhere are buzzing. A new play is opening at The Stage. You waddle over to the Plaza and stand underneath the bright lights of the theater's marquee. You then go inside and sit back in your plush red velvet seat, waiting for the show to begin.

From acting to special effects to costumes, the show is amazing! Afterward, you stand up and cheer. It was another great play at The Stage!

In this book, you are going to get a special, behind-the-scenes tour of The Stage and all the shows that go on there. From acting to ticket sales to simply enjoying the show, there's a way for everyone to lend a flipper at The Stage.

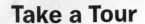

STAGE SECRETS

I'm a penguin who has a passion for The Stage. When a new production comes out, I put on my director's cap and get ready to lead my pals in a stellar show. I'm going to be telling you fun facts and secrets about The Stage throughout this book. Whenever you see my picture, get ready to learn something new about The Stage!

Theater Seats:
Kick back and watch the show in these comfy chairs.

Switchbox 3000:
Click the buttons and pull the levers to control the sets, turn on spotlights, and create special effects.

SWITCHBOX

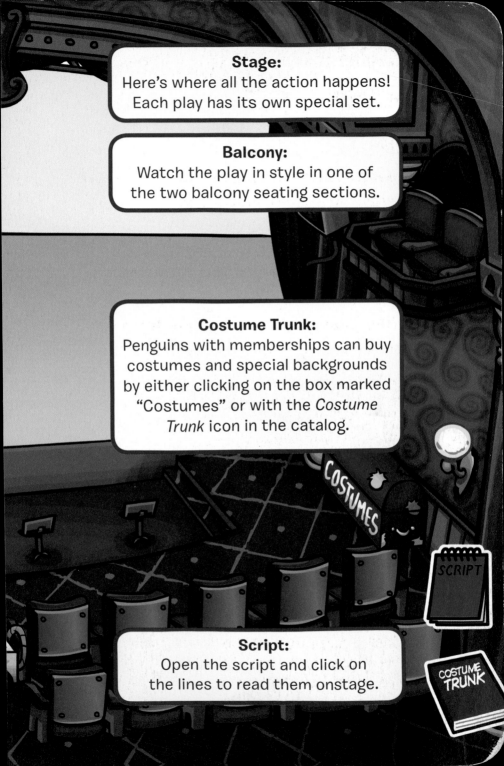

Stage:
Here's where all the action happens!
Each play has its own special set.

Balcony:
Watch the play in style in one of
the two balcony seating sections.

Costume Trunk:
Penguins with memberships can buy
costumes and special backgrounds
by either clicking on the box marked
"Costumes" or with the *Costume
Trunk* icon in the catalog.

COSTUMES

SCRIPT

Script:
Open the script and click on
the lines to read them onstage.

COSTUME
TRUNK

How to Put on a Show

While an audience is always needed to watch and appreciate the plays that are performed at The Stage, a lot of work goes into putting on a wonderful show. Here's how you can make it happen.

Cast and Crew Needed

Whether you've dreamed of acting, directing, or working behind the scenes on a show, The Stage is the perfect place to show off your special talents.

To get started, you'll need penguins to play all the parts in the show. Let your friends know you want to put on a show. One way to spread the word is by sending a postcard through Penguin Mail.

Putting on a play is also a great way to make new friends. Many of the penguins hanging out at The Stage want to be involved in a production. Ask around. You'll be saying, "Places, please!" before you know it!

Lend a Flipper

So you've got your crew assembled? It's time to pick jobs to help out with the production. There are plenty of fun jobs at The Stage. Here are just a few of them.

Director

It's a good idea to pick who will be the director first. The director is in charge of the production and can help decide who should do which jobs. You can buy a director's cap in the *Costume Trunk*. The script has lines in it for the director to say, too.

Actor

Want to act? Pick up a script and hit The Stage! You can volunteer for the role you want. Or, the director can hold an audition. Read lines from the script, and the director can pick the best penguin for the role.

Usher

Escort penguins to their seats before the big performance and show them how to get into the balcony.

Ticket Taker

Walk into the ticket booth in the front of the theater and ask penguins if they'd like a ticket to the show.

Orchestra

Live music makes any show more exciting. If you own an instrument, get together with other musicians. Set up in the black area in front of The Stage and turn the play into a musical!

Play Promoter

Spread the word about your play around Club Penguin. Make sure to tell everyone the time and location of the play.

Audience Member

Every production needs an audience. Sit back and enjoy the show. Make sure to let other penguins know if you like the show by using your emotes. As an audience member, you can also work the Switchbox 3000 to turn the spotlights on and reveal secret set actions during the play.

Practice Makes Perfect

Now that everyone has a job, it's time to start practicing. The director can pick a time for everyone to rehearse. The actors can run through their lines, and the stagehands can practice hitting the switches at the right time. Keep at it until you've got a perfect production! Then set a time for everyone to meet for the real show.

Roll Out the Red Carpet

Before the big show, why not have a fancy red-carpet premiere? Ask all the cast and crew to meet outside the theater dressed in their best outfits. Get other penguins in on the fun by asking them to be reporters and photographers. They can interview the stars of the show and pretend to snap pictures.

Lights, Camera, Action

Once the audience is seated, it's time to begin. Don't be nervous. Just do your best!

Afterparty

After the applause has died down, it's time to celebrate your success. Host a party for the cast and crew at your igloo, or have everyone get together at the Iceberg, the Pizza Parlor, or the Coffee Shop. Make sure to thank everyone for their hard work.

There's More!

Haven't had enough play action yet? Read on to find out about many of the plays that have been performed on The Stage—with lots of ideas for recreating them anytime, anywhere!

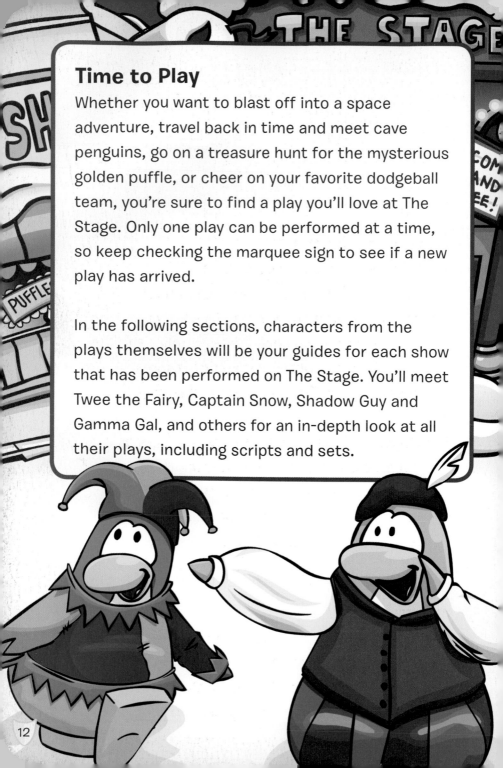

Time to Play

Whether you want to blast off into a space adventure, travel back in time and meet cave penguins, go on a treasure hunt for the mysterious golden puffle, or cheer on your favorite dodgeball team, you're sure to find a play you'll love at The Stage. Only one play can be performed at a time, so keep checking the marquee sign to see if a new play has arrived.

In the following sections, characters from the plays themselves will be your guides for each show that has been performed on The Stage. You'll meet Twee the Fairy, Captain Snow, Shadow Guy and Gamma Gal, and others for an in-depth look at all their plays, including scripts and sets.

DIY Guide

Using the scripts for each play that are provided in this book, you can put on a Club Penguin play anytime! These Do-It-Yourself sections have great suggestions, too.

Costume Creator

No *Costume Trunk*? No problem! We'll give you tips to make your own costumes. You can also come up with great costume ideas all on your own. Look through your closet and dig out old Halloween costumes. You never know what might come in handy.

The Costume Creator will also tell you how to use paper, crayons, and tape to make costume accessories. Always make sure to ask for an adult's help or permission when using scissors, glue, paint, or other craft items.

Make a Scene

Recreate play sets anywhere with these fun, easy instructions. Remember, you can always keep it simple. You don't need an elaborate set to put on a great show.

What's Your Penguin Play Personality?

Which Club Penguin play was made for you to take a starring role in? Take the penguin play personality quiz now to find out.

1. What would you rather do?

a. Tell jokes
b. Dance
c. Search for the latest pin
d. Find out about Gary the Gadget Guy's latest inventions
e. Play games

2. What do your buddies like best about you?

a. You are always making them laugh.
b. You know how to cheer them up when they are feeling down.
c. If they have a problem, you'll help them solve it.
d. You've always got the latest gadgets at your igloo.
e. They know hanging out with you will always be an adventure!

3. If you had to pick one of the following games to play, it would be:

a. *Catchin' Waves*

b. *Dance Contest*

c. *Card-Jitsu*

d. *Astro-Barrier*

e. *Jet Pack Adventure*

4. My favorite Club Penguin hangout is:

a. The Stage

b. The Night Club

c. The Dojo

d. HQ

e. Wherever the action is at!

5. Which penguin would you most like to meet?

a. Any of the members of the Club Penguin Band

b. Cadence

c. Sensei

d. Gary the Gadget Guy

e. Captain Rockhopper

Your Penguin Play Personality Quiz Results

If you answered mostly As: You'll have the audience rolling in the aisles in comedies like *Fairy Fables* or *The Twelfth Fish*.

If you answered mostly Bs: Upbeat plays like *Team Blue's Rally Debut* and its sequels were made for penguins like you.

If you answered mostly Cs: A smart, determined penguin like you would make a great Detective Hammer in the mystery *Ruby and the Ruby*.

If you answered mostly Ds: You're a dreamer who will love taking a step into the future or the past in *Space Adventure*, *Space Adventure Planet Y*, or *The Penguins That Time Forgot*.

If you answered mostly Es: You'll find the adventure you love in plays like *Quest for the Golden Puffle* and *Squidzoid vs Shadow Guy & Gamma Gal*.

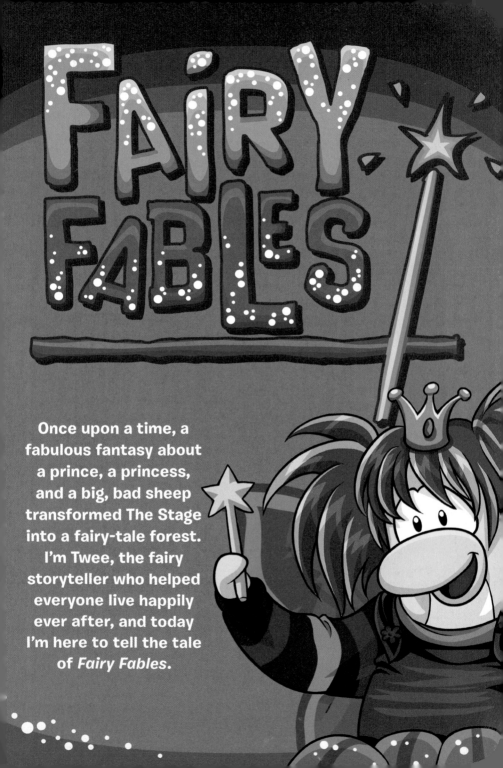

FAIRY FABLES

Once upon a time, a fabulous fantasy about a prince, a princess, and a big, bad sheep transformed The Stage into a fairy-tale forest. I'm Twee, the fairy storyteller who helped everyone live happily ever after, and today I'm here to tell the tale of *Fairy Fables*.

The Characters

Twee
I live in a magical library where I love to share stories of my adventures.

Prince Redhood
Don't be fooled by the name. This charming prince isn't too fond of the color red.

Big Bad Wool
This sheep is misunderstood. He only wants something to eat, but he's got to blow down a few trees to get it.

Princess Grumpunzel
They don't call her *Grumpunzel* for nothing. This is one grumpy princess!

STAGE SECRETS

When The Stage was built, a yellow puffle was hiding in the balcony. You could make him appear by moving your mouse over the two puffles on the wooden plaque on the top of The Stage. Ever since, the yellow puffle has made a special appearance in every play. Check the set closely for any sign of The Stage's special puffle.

The Story

Our tale began when Prince Redhood decided to set out through the forest to bring some croissants to the long-haired Princess Grumpunzel. Along the way, he encountered a scary sheep called the Big Bad Wool. Like any good fairy should, I gave the hero some advice that saved the day.

The Set

You can create all kinds of special effects on this set with the Switchbox 3000. The coolest functions include causing a unicorn set piece to descend from the ceiling, and knocking a book from the bookshelf to the floor, causing a plant to grow out of the pages.

Fairy Fables: The Script

Twee: Once upon a time, a prince dressed all in red . . .

Redhood: Red?! Are you sure? It's not really my color.

Twee: Don't interrupt! I said he was dressed in RED!

Redhood: Oh. All right, then. What a lovely day!

Twee: He was taking croissants to a hungry princess.

Redhood: Golly, I hope she likes pastries.

Twee: But suddenly, something jumped out of the forest!

Redhood: Oh no! A scary-looking sheep!

Big Bad Wool: *BAA!* I'm the Big Bad Wool and I'm hungry!

Redhood: What great big teeth you've got!

Big Bad Wool: All the better to eat croissants with!

Redhood: Not a chance, Woolly! They're for the princess!

Big Bad Wool: Then I'll huff and I'll puff . . .

Twee: And the Big Bad Wool blew all the trees down.

Redhood: Oh no! What am I going to do?

Twee: You need to distract the sheep, of course!

Redhood: Oh yes. Look over there!

Big Bad Wool: A unicorn flying through the sky? *BAA-zaa!*

Redhood: Aha, now I can escape!

Twee: Finally the prince arrived at the castle.

Redhood: Now I will climb up Grumpunzel's long hair.

Twee: You'll have to make do with a ladder.

Redhood: If I must . . .

Grumpunzel: La la la la . . .

Redhood: She's totally lost in la-la land. What do I do now?

Twee: Throw a magic snowball at her, of course!

Redhood throws a snowball at Grumpunzel.

Grumpunzel: What do you think you're doing?

Redhood: Princess! I've brought you some croissants.

Grumpunzel: Croissants? I asked for COOKIES!

Redhood: Guess they don't call her Grumpunzel for nothing.

Twee: I think she should go back to la-la land. *ZAP!*

Big Bad Wool: *BAA!* Excuse me! I'm really hungry here!

Twee: Well, there are plenty of croissants to go 'round.

Redhood: You'd better not wool them all down at once.

Twee: And they all lived happily ever after.

THE END

Create your own happy ending with these tips!

Costume Creator

Twee: To make a crown, cut a strip of paper to go around your head, and cut a zigzag shape on one edge. Then glue together and decorate! To make Twee's wand, cut out a paper star. Glue or tape it onto the end of a drinking straw.

Prince Redhood: Glue a white feather onto a red cap. If you don't have a red cape lying around, a red towel or sheet will do the job.

Big Bad Wool: A white sweatshirt or T-shirt makes a great sheep costume. To get a woolly look, tape cotton balls all over your garment.

Grumpunzel: A dress can turn anyone into a princess. Try using yarn or rope to make Grumpunzel's braid.

Make a Scene

Build Twee's library with a chair and some books. Take the play outside for a naturally enchanted forest or use houseplants to create the forest.

THE PENGUINS THAT TIME FORGOT

My name is Chester and I've always been a curious penguin. So when a penguin offered to sell me a time machine for only ten coins, I jumped at the chance. I couldn't help but wonder where I might end up. Unfortunately for me, I found out this time machine only offered a one-way trip.

The Characters

Chester the Time Traveler
I wanted to travel back in time and I did. Be careful what you wish for!

Kek
Is this cave penguin hungry? All he talks about is grub.

Critteroo
This cave penguin tried to warn me about the lava flowing from the volcano.

Tiki
Maybe one day I'll understand what Tiki is saying. After all, I'm not leaving anytime soon!

STAGE SECRETS

Actors can be very superstitious. Many consider it bad luck to wish a performer "good luck" before a show. If you want to offer a word of support, say "break a leg" instead. It might not sound lucky, but it's the traditional way of wishing someone well in the theater!

The Story

The Time Travel 1000—what a machine! Or so I thought. I couldn't wait to travel back in time. So I put on the time travel hat and climbed into the Time Travel 1000. When I got out, I was surrounded by cave penguins, dinosaurs, and an erupting volcano! Oh no! What would become of me?

The Set

Use the Switchbox 3000 to make dinosaurs move and see new ones appear. You can also control the time machine and change the color of the lava.

The Penguins That Time Forgot: The Script

Chester: Time to try out this new Time Travel 1000!

Critteroo: UGG! DINO! UGG!

Chester: What is this place? Where am I?

Kek: GRUB! GRUB GRUB!

Chester: I'm in Grub? What's a Grub?

Critteroo: LAVA! LAVA!

Chester: Lava?! I've gotta get out of here!

Time machine breaks.

Chester: Great, now I'm stuck in some place called Grub.

Tiki: TIKI UGG!

Kek: GRRRRRRRUB!

Chester: Now who's this with the big, silly mask?

Tiki: TIKI TIKI BOARD TIKI BOARD!

Critteroo: TIKI! TIKI ATOOK!

Tiki: ABOOT! ABOOT!

Kek: YUB NUB GRUB!

Chester: Okay, really now. Can't you just use real words?

Critteroo: GRUB! TIKI GRUB-GRUB!

Chester: You do know you don't make any sense, right?

Critteroo: LAVA NO TIKI GRUB!

Chester: Sigh. Okay, something about lava and grubs.

Tiki: ABOOOOOOT!

Chester: You were wearing boots, but the grubs took them?

Kek: LAVA NO LAVA! GRUB TIKI GRUB!

Chester: Let me guess, your name is Tiki, and you're Grub.

Tiki: ABOOT TIKI!

Critteroo: TIKI GRUB-GRUB!

Chester: I give up! I have no idea what you're saying.

Kek: DINO YUB NUB LAVAAA!

Chester: Well, I may as well join in . . .

Chester: GRUB GRUB!

Tiki: TIKI BOARD BOARD!

Kek: LAVA DINO GRUB!

Chester: Last time I buy a time machine for ten coins . . .

The End

The Penguins That Time Forgot: DIY

Take a trip back in time when you stage your own production of *The Penguins That Time Forgot*.

Costume Creator

Chester: A hat can be turned into a time-traveling wonder. Draw two clock faces on paper, cut them out, and tape them onto the hat.

Kek and Critteroo: The unibrow look was popular with cave penguins. Get permission to use makeup or face paint to give yourself one big eyebrow.

Tiki: Tape together enough green paper to fit around your waist. Draw a tiki mask on paper. Cut it out, adding eye holes. Attach string to tie around your head.

Make a Scene

Use a large cardboard box to make a time machine. Write "Time Travel 1000" on one side and draw a clock on the other. Lay it on its side and open the flaps so time travelers can take a trip. A red towel or sheet can be a stream of lava. Scatter dinosaur toys around the set or draw some on paper and tape them to the wall. Houseplants and rocks will give your play a prehistoric feel.

QUEST FOR THE GOLDEN PUFFLE

Danger? No problem! I'm Alaska, a daring treasure hunter who travels the world searching for rare puffles. With my trusty sidekick, Yukon, by my side, I've faced down mummies and crocodiles. I'm going to share with you one of my greatest adventures yet—the *Quest for the Golden Puffle.*

The Characters

Alaska
I love puffles and adventures—and I won't stop searching for either!

Yukon
Yukon may be a bit on the timid side, but I couldn't find a more loyal friend to aid me on my quests.

Boris
Boris is a chocolate-loving mummy who wasn't very happy when I snuck into his pyramid.

King Ra-Ra
Once ruler of the lost Gold Wrapper Empire, King Ra-Ra now resides in the Great Pyramid.

The Story

Yukon and I set out to find the golden puffle at the Great Pyramid. All the traps along the way didn't stop us. Then we spotted the golden puffle. But suddenly, Boris and King Ra-Ra appeared. When Boris unwrapped the golden puffle, revealing it was only made of chocolate, I was disappointed. But I'll find the golden puffle one day!

The Set

The Switchbox 3000 sets off traps by collapsing the bridges and causing part of the statue to fall. It also uncovers secrets like hidden doors.

"Onward to victory and the rarest puffles!"
—Alaska

Quest for the Golden Puffle: The Script

Yukon: We have to be careful in this pyramid, Alaska!

Alaska: Can't find rare puffles without a little danger . . . Hey, look, a switch! Wonder what it does . . .

Yukon: Oh no! Run! It's a snowball trap!

Alaska: What's an adventure without a few traps?

Yukon: That was close! Told you we should be careful!

Alaska: Careful is my middle name.

Yukon: Look! The golden puffle! Let's get it!

Alaska: I've been waiting a long, long time for this . . .

Door opens and Boris appears.

Boris: TUMMMMMMY!

King Ra-Ra: Halt! Who dares to enter the Great Pyramid?

Alaska: Quick, Yukon! Grab the golden puffle!

Yukon: Got it! Let's get out of here!

Boris: TUMMMMMMMMY!

King Ra-Ra: Don't let them take it, Boris!

Alaska: We've gotta get out of here . . . fast!

Yukon: Oh no! We're trapped in the pyramid!

Alaska: You can say that again.

Yukon: Oh no! We're trapped in the pyramid!

Boris: TUMMMMMMMMMMY!

King Ra-Ra: You can't escape the Great Pyramid! Now give us the golden puffle!

Alaska: I don't give up my quests that easily, Ra-Ra!

Boris: TUMMMMMMY!

Yukon: Wait! I think I know how to stop all of this!

Yukon gives Boris the golden puffle.

Boris: TUM MEEEEE!

Alaska: What are you doing, Yukon?! That's my treasure!

Boris unwraps the Golden Puffle.

Yukon: It's a puffle-shaped chocolate in a gold wrapper!

King Ra-Ra: That's right! And Boris was really hungry!

Boris: YUMMMMMMMY!

King Ra-Ra: That's why we had to get it back!

Alaska: Sigh. Guess it's not the rare puffle I thought.

King Ra-Ra: Oh, but it is rare! It is made of the island's rarest dark chocolate!

Yukon: These weren't the puffles we were looking for.

Alaska: Do not fear, Yukon! New adventures await!

King Ra-Ra: Hmmm . . . where did I put that snowball of mine?

Alaska: Onward to victory and the rarest puffles!

Boris: THAT'S A WRAP!

THE END

Brave the pyramid and search for the rarest puffle.

Costume Creator

Alaska and Yukon: A brown hat of any sort will work for Alaska and Yukon. To complete the look, wear a button-down shirt and khaki pants or jeans with a big belt. A piece of rope can be used for Alaska's lasso. Use an old backpack for Yukon's supply bag.

Boris: Wear white clothing. Wrap a roll of bath tissue around yourself for the full mummy effect.

King Ra-Ra: Cut the inner circle out of a paper plate for King Ra-Ra's collar. Decorate the plate in red, blue, and gold. Wear a white skirt or sheet around your waist, gold bracelets, and sandals.

Make a Scene

If you have a sandbox, bring the play outdoors. If not, use beige towels as your sandy floor. Blue towels can make the river. Use a flattened cardboard box as the bridge between the desert and the river. For the inside of the pyramid, draw hieroglyphics on paper and hang them on the wall.

The name's Hammer—
Jacque Hammer.
If there's a mystery,
I'm the penguin to solve
it. I've cracked many
cases, but there is one
I'll never forget. It all
started when a penguin
walked into my office
one dark and
stormy day . . .

The Characters

Jacque Hammer
I'm a tough private detective who has a nose for sniffing out trouble.

Ruby
A beautiful and glamorous penguin, Ruby can be a bit careless with her precious gemstones.

Tenor
Tenor was playing hopscotch when her gemstone went missing—
or was he?

Dom
Dom is a helpful doorman.

The Story

When Ruby suspected her valuable ruby had been stolen, she turned to me to track her gemstone down for her. Armed with my wits alone, I questioned suspects and left no fish unturned in my search for the missing gemstone. Persistence paid off. I found it. Another day in the life of Jacque Hammer, another crime solved.

The Set

Instead of a Switchbox 3000, the hints in the script lead penguins to click on objects such as the filing cabinet, trash can, a book, vase, painting, and safe. Doing this not only leads to Ruby's missing gemstone but a hidden ruby pin!

STAGE SECRETS

Move your mouse over all the images in the *Costume Trunk* to search for secret items. A dark detective coat and a black-and-white player card background were once hidden in *Ruby and the Ruby*'s Costume Trunk. It took real detective work to locate them. They were very hard to find!

Ruby and the Ruby: The Script

SCENE 1

Hammer: I was working late. A terrible storm was raging.

Ruby: You've got to help me!

Hammer: What's the problem, madam?

Ruby: Someone has stolen my gemstone!

Hammer: Jacque Hammer, at your service.

Ruby: Let's work together.

Hammer: I work alone, Ms. Ruby.

Ruby: There was this fishy-looking guy outside.

Hammer: And you suspect him?

Ruby: I saw him throw something in the bin . . .

SCENE 2

Hammer: The name's Hammer, Jacque Hammer. I got a few questions for you.

Tenor: Mind if I play hopscotch while you ask them?

Hammer: What were you doing yesterday?

Tenor: I was right here with my hopscotch gang.

Hammer: I bet you've hopscotched away a few gems, right?

Tenor: You're barking up the wrong tree, Hammer.

SCENE 3

Hammer: There was nothing in the bin. I needed clues.

Dom: Hello, Mr. Hammer. It's good to see you, sir.

Hammer: Seen anything suspicious, Dom?

Dom: Sorry, Mr. Hammer, sir. I haven't.

Hammer: Where's Ms. Ruby?

Dom: She's arranging flowers across the hall, sir.

Hammer: That lady's trouble. I need to speak with her . . .

Dom: Don't forget to sign the guestbook, sir.

SCENE 4

Hammer: Anything else you can tell me, madam?

Ruby: Haven't you found it yet? I'm busy.

Ruby exits.

Hammer: I found a note under a vase. The numbers look like a combination.

SCENE 5

Hammer: Here's your gem, Ms. Ruby. It was safe all along.

Ruby: Oh, jolly, well done, Hammer.

Hammer: Another day, another crime solved.

THE END

Feeling mysterious? Stump your audience with your very own production of *Ruby and the Ruby*.

Costume Creator

Jacque Hammer: Look like the cool detective with a trench coat or raincoat and a fedora-style hat. Carry a magnifying glass to complete the outfit.

Ruby: Glam it up with a fancy dress and necklace.

Tenor: Dress up like Tenor with a suit and tie.

Dom: Wear a fancy shirt or jacket, especially if it has big, shiny buttons. Add a hat to top it off.

Make a Scene

A chair and a desk or table is all you need for Hammer's office. Draw a hopscotch board on cardboard for Tenor's alley scene. Use regular furniture for Ruby's house.

Turn your home into a real-life mystery. Hide the "ruby" (it could be a bead, rock, or anything at all) and the actors can look for it, just like in the play!

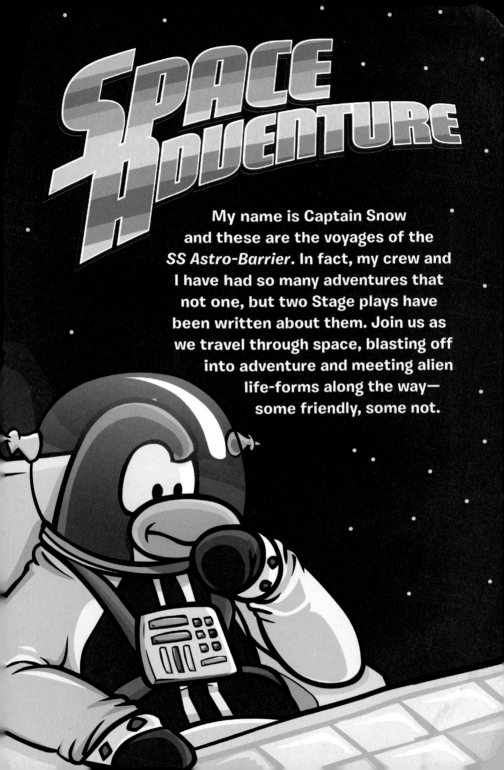

SPACE ADVENTURE

My name is Captain Snow
and these are the voyages of the
SS *Astro-Barrier*. In fact, my crew and
I have had so many adventures that
not one, but two Stage plays have
been written about them. Join us as
we travel through space, blasting off
into adventure and meeting alien
life-forms along the way—
some friendly, some not.

The Characters

Captain Snow
Every spaceship needs a clever and fearless captain. Crash landings and angry aliens don't scare me!

Ensign
My trusty ensign remains cool and calm under pressure.

Tin Can 3000
Tin Can 3000 is a robot that alerts the crew to any signs of danger.

Zip
When the *SS Astro-Barrier* crash-landed on Planet X, we weren't sure if this alien was a friend or foe.

Quip and Qua
Are two brains better than one? These aliens tried to turn Tin Can 3000 against us and steal the *SS Astro-Barrier*.

STAGE SECRETS

The first play to debut on The Stage was *Space Adventure*!

The Story

Our story began in *Space Adventure*. We were heading to Planet X in search of alien life when we crash-landed. But life on Planet X turned out to be friendly.

Unfortunately, on our next adventure, in the play *Space Adventure Planet Y*, we were not so lucky. Would we come up with a plan to escape?

The Set

With the Switchbox 3000, you can crash-land the spaceship and cause a hovering robot probe to fly through the set. You can also make the vacuum robot clean up a mess and make the yellow puffle appear in a small flying saucer.

Space Adventure: The Script

Captain: Captain's journal, entry number eleven-sixteen . . . We're flying toward Planet X to find alien life.

Ensign: Speed set to carp two, ready to land.

Tin Can 3000: *TWEEP!* ERROR 500 . . . ENGINE FAILING!

Captain: Ensign, increase emergency power!

Ensign: Already used up all backup power, sir!

Tin Can 3000: *GLEEEEEP!* ENGINE HAS STOPPED . . . NO POWER LEFT!

Captain: Prepare the survey team to investigate.

Ensign: Captain, receiving a signal off the port bow.

Captain: Tin Can 3000, what do you know about Planet X?

Tin Can 3000: ERROR 404! NO RECORDS FOUND!

Zip jumps out of alien spaceship.

Zip: Halt! I am Zip, ruler of Planet X. Who are you?

Captain: I am Captain Snow and this is my crew.

Ensign: We came from Club Penguin, but our ship broke.

Captain: Zip, we need your help to rebuild our engine.

Zip: I don't just fix any old ship that lands here.

Tin Can 3000: CONNECTION . . . REFUSED BY HOST. . .

Ensign: But without our spaceship we can't get home!

Zip: Did you try clearing the ship computer's cache?

Ensign: Wait! I didn't! Thanks for the help. I'll try it!

Ensign and Tin Can 3000 work on spaceship's computer.

Tin Can 3000: ENGINES OPERATIONAL . . . *TWEEP!*

Captain: Thank you for your excellent help, Zip!

Zip: Wait! Can I go with you?

Tin Can 3000: *BLEEB!* ERROR 407! REQUEST MORE DETAILS!

Ensign: Why do you want to go to Club Penguin?

Zip: My home isn't the same since the others left!

Ensign: Well, we'd love to have you on Club Penguin.

Captain: You have my permission to join us aboard, Zip. Ensign, set a course for the Plaza. Carp five!

Ensign: Engines set for destination, Captain!

Captain: Let's get back to Club Penguin with our new friend!

All: HOORAY FOR CLUB PENGUIN!

THE END

Space Adventure Planet Y: The Script

Captain: Captain's journal, entry number thirty-sixteen . . . The *SS Astro-Barrier* returns to Club Penguin . . .

Ensign: Speed set to carp five.

Zip: Wait! Watch out for the—

Asteroid hits the SS Astro-Barrier.

Tin Can 3000: *TWEEE-BEEP!* ERROR 6000! DIRECT HIT!

Zip: . . . asteroid!

Ensign: Captain, it's thrown us off course!

Captain: Engage the carp drive. Full reverse!

Tin Can 3000: *BEEP BEEP!* CARP DRIVE FAILURE.

Ensign: Negative, Captain. It's not working.

Zip: Have you tried clearing the cache?

Ensign: I've tried, but it won't reload!

Captain: Emergency crash landing—that planet will do.

Tin Can 3000: *GLEEEEEEP!* OVERHEATING!

Zip: No, not Planet Y! My rivals, the Qs, live here!

Ship crashes into building.

Qua: Visitors, you've disturbed our meeting . . .

Quip: So you have our old robot, Tin Can. Greetings.

Qua: We're planning to make a giant spacecraft.

Quip: Tin Can 3000, help us get ship parts. Now!

Tin Can 3000: NEW ORDER RECEIVED. REPROGRAMMING.

Zip: Wait! Remember space directive 402?

Captain: The bot exchange agreement! Quick thinking, Zip!

Quip: They own the bot. He can't destroy the craft . . .

Qua: Let's do it ourselves—we'll be fast!

Zip: Restart the bot, and let's get out of here.

Tin Can 3000: REBOOTING. REBOOTING. REBOOTING. *GLEEEP!* ENGINE TERMINATED. JET FUEL LOW!

Ensign: No! How are we going to get back this time?

Tin Can 3000: *ZWEEEP!* ABORT, RETRY, FAIL?

Captain: Retry. Tin Can, use ice cream for fuel.

Zip: It's working! Let's get out of here.

Captain: Set a course for the Iceberg. Carp five. Engage!

Quip: We shall meet again, Captain Snow . . .

THE END

Space Adventure: DIY

**Blast off into your own production
of *Space Adventure*!**

Costume Creator

Captain Snow and Ensign: To make a space
helmet, find a box that fits on your head. Cut a
hole for your face.

Tin Can 3000: Find a box that will fit over your
head. Cut a hole for your face. Next, find a box big
enough to fit over your body. Cut holes for your
neck and arms. Cover both boxes in foil.

Zip: Get permission to use green face paint. If you
have white and black makeup, draw a third eye in
the middle of your forehead.

Quip and Qua: Wear blue. Find an old cap and get
permission to draw a brain on it. Wear it backward.

Make a Scene

Use chairs and tables for the inside of the *SS
Astro-Barrier*. Draw computer screens and control
knobs on paper and get permission to tape them
to the wall. Chairs and a table are all you need for
Quip and Qua's conference room.

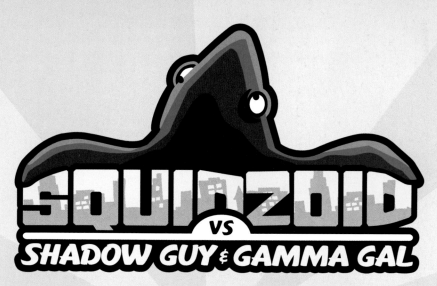

SQUIDZOID
VS
SHADOW GUY & GAMMA GAL

We're Shadow Guy and Gamma Gal, the dynamic duo you turn to when the forces of evil are on the loose and villainous villains are wreaking havoc. You'll never know when we're around. We look like any other penguins until trouble erupts. Then we transform into our superhero costumes and rush in to save the day!

The Characters

Shadow Guy
I'm a "dark" defender bringing justice wherever I go. Villains, watch out for my Shadow Wave!

Gamma Gal
I'm a pink powerhouse who really packs a punch. My Plasma Glow Wave will put bad guys to a stop!

Squidzoid
Standing over 100 feet tall, this monster appears without warning, destroying everything in its path.

Mild-Mannered Reporter
A true journalist, nothing will stop this reporter from covering the news—not even a gigantic squid!

Witness
This random penguin just happens to witness the epic battle between us superheroes and the monster.

The Story

It's not every day that a gigantic monster shows up on the island and eats the Pet Shop. Quicker than you can say, "Here they come to save the day," we changed into our superhero costumes and prepared to put a stop to Squidzoid's rampage. Would we be able to save Club Penguin?

The Set

Use the Switchbox 3000 to set off explosions and shoot laser beams. Or change the play from day to night and send a car smashing into the giant robot.

STAGE SECRETS

Wearing the superhero mask, costume, and cape of Shadow Guy or Gamma Gal, click the blue penguin in the toolbar on the bottom of the page. Then wave to glow like Gamma Gal or use Shadow Guy's Shadow Wave!

Squidzoid vs Shadow Guy & Gamma Gal: The Script

Reporter: Action news live! Tell us what's happening!

Witness: I saw a monster eat the Pet Shop.

Squidzoid: *GRAWL!* HUNGRY!

Witness: Who can save us now?

Shadow Guy: The city needs our help.

Gamma Gal: Super costume mega transform!

Witness: Look! The heroes have arrived!

Reporter: Here they come to save the day!

Shadow Guy: Freeze Squidzoid! Drop that shop!

Gamma Gal: I think you've had enough to eat!

Squidzoid: *BLARRG!* YOU CAN'T STOP ME!

Gamma Gal: Oh yeah? Take this! PLASMA GLOW WAVE!

Squidzoid: *RROOOOOAAAARR!*

Reporter: The superheroes are using their powers!

Witness: Hooray, heroes! Nice going!

Squidzoid: PUNY HEROES! YOU'RE NO MATCH FOR ME!

Shadow Guy: Then try this on for size. SHADOW WAVE!

Squidzoid: *GLEEGRRAWLL!*

Reporter: This just in! Squidzoid is trying to escape!

Witness: After it! Don't let it get away!

Gamma Gal: Quick! With our powers combined!

Shadow Guy: For great justice!

Squidzoid: NO! THIS IS IMPOSSIBLE! *GRRAAA!*

Witness: It's turning into a penguin!

Squidzoid: Hey, I'm a penguin again. What happened?

Reporter: You turned into Squidzoid!

Witness: And started eating the city!

Squidzoid: Oh! I had a monster appetite!

Shadow Guy: With great power comes great hunger.

Gamma Gal: Looks like our work here is done!

Squidzoid: Let's go get a fish pizza.

Reporter: The city is saved! This reporter is signing off.

THE END

Squidzoid vs Shadow Guy & Gamma Gal: DIY

Feeling like a superhero? Put your powers on display with these do-it-yourself tips.

Costume Creator

Shadow Guy and Gamma Gal: Draw a mask onto blue or pink paper. Cut it out, including holes for your eyes and on each side. Attach string through the holes and tie around your head. For the cape, a blue or pink shirt or pillowcase can be safety-pinned, with your parents' help, to your shirt.

Squidzoid: Start with a blue shirt. For the tentacles, paper towel rolls can be colored blue and clipped onto the bottom of the sweatshirt. Old panty hose or tights, stuffed with tissue paper, can also make convincing tentacles.

Reporter: Grab a camera. You're ready to report!

Witness: No costume necessary.

Make a Scene

Stage the epic battle with these simple ideas. Use any toy houses or models you might have lying around. Or break out the crayons and pencils and transform ordinary boxes into buildings!

TEAM BLUE vs TEAM RED

Let me hear you say MOOOOOOSE! I'm Zeus, the moose mascot for Team Blue. It's my job to get the audience pumped up and cheering. But I wasn't always this confident. In *Team Blue's Rally Debut*, I met some cool mascots who helped me get over my stage fright. And in *Team Blue's Rally 2*, I had to take on Team Red all by myself. Go, Team Blue!

The Characters

Zeus
I'm just an ordinary penguin who transforms into an energetic mascot when I put on my costume.

Peppy
Any cool birds in the house?
There are when this parrot mascot is around!

Tate
This pirate ship mascot could be a little more graceful. Tate's known to trip and fall a lot.

The Judges
It's a tough job for the judges to decide the winner of the mascot tryouts!

Jupiter
Check out Team Red's new mascot. It's a moose! Wonder where they got that idea from . . .

Bella
Bella is a peppy cheerleader who is rooting for Team Red.

Jeff
Jeff is the referee of the dodgeball game. He wants everyone to be good sports and play fair.

Scarlet
Head of Team Red, Scarlet is unstoppable on the court, and she never messes up her hair.

Eric
Silent. Skilled. Perfect. Eric the Red is known for his intense abilities. He's even rumored to have ninja training.

Team Blue and Team Red Members
You can't have a dodgeball game without the players!

The Story

Time for the big mascot tryouts! In *Team Blue's Rally Debut*, I got really scared for my audition. I didn't want to look silly, so I decided not to go on. Peppy and Tate, the other mascots, encouraged me and said they would try out with me. At that moment, we became Team Blue! The crowd went wild and all three of us were the winners of the mascot tryouts.

In *Team Blue's Rally 2*, I faced a tough crowd at a dodgeball game without Peppy and Tate. I didn't expect Team Red to have a moose mascot, too! I was trying to be a good sport but Jupiter, Team Red's mascot, wasn't interested in a friendly game. It was time to do what I do best— pump up the audience and get them cheering. Go, Team Blue!

In *Team Blue vs Team Red*, the two teams went head-to-head once again—this time with new fierce Team Red opponents Scarlet and Eric. Though it wasn't easy, could I use my mascot skills to help Team Blue tie up the score?

A few years ago, the Pet Shop and Pizza Parlor were the only buildings in the Plaza. Construction began on The Stage, and a sign saying "Actors Wanted" went up. In November 2007, construction was complete and penguins have been shining onstage ever since.

STAGE SECRETS

The Set

Open lockers and create cool special effects for each of the mascots with the Switchbox 3000!

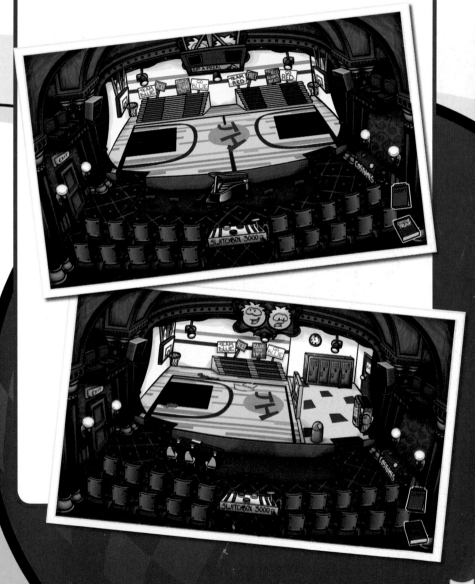

Team Blue's Rally Debut: The Script

Happy Judge: Welcome, everyone, to the big Mascot Tryouts!

Grumpy Judge: Each mascot has to get through us to win.

Cheerleader: Let's give 'em a big round of applause!

Audience: Yeah! Go, Team Blue!

Happy Judge: Give it up for PEPPPPPPPYYYYYYY!

Peppy: ANY COOL BIRDS IN THE HOUSE TODAY? LEMME HEAR YA SAY BRRRRRRRRRD!

Audience: BRRRRRRRRRD!

Peppy: OH EE OH EE OH!

Audience: ICE! ICE! ICE!

Tate: Did somebody say ICE!? Oops! Didn't see those bleachers there . . .

Cheerleader: Everyone give it up for Tate! GO, BLUE!

Grumpy Judge: Man, this competition is soooo lame.

Zeus: Oh, man! I don't want to go out there!

Tate: C'mon, you should go. You'll do better than me.

Zeus: But I don't even have a cool entrance!

Peppy: HEY! TURN THOSE FROWNS UPSIDE DOWN! DON'T LEAVE ME TO BE THE CLOWN!

Zeus: But Peppy . . . I don't want to look dumb!

Grumpy Judge: Excuse me, but can we get on with the show?

Tate: You couldn't do any worse than me, Zeus!

Audience: WE WANT ZEUS! WE WANT ZEUS!

Tate: See, Zeus! They want to see your cool outfit!

Peppy: YEAH, ZEUS, GIVE 'EM THE SCHOOL SPIRIT!

Zeus: I just don't want to be alone out there.

Peppy: WELL, WHY DIDN'T YOU SAY SO!

Zeus: What do you mean?

Peppy: LET'S GO TOGETHER! AS A TEAM!

Tate: Yeah! We can be the Team Blue Crew!

Zeus: Okay . . . maybe that would work . . . let's try it!

Peppy: BLUE . . . TEAM . . . BACK AGAIN! TIME IS RIGHT SO LET'S BEGIN!

Peppy: STOP! . . . . BLUE TIME!

Tate: Make some noise for the Team Blue Crew!

Zeus: Let me hear ya say MOOOOOOSE!

Audience: MOOOOOOOSE!

Tate: Let me hear ya say ICE!

Audience: BERG!

Tate: ICE!

Audience: BERG!

Cheerleader: Looks like the audience likes ALL OF THEM!

Grumpy Judge: Umm . . . can we choose none of them?

Happy Judge: Presenting the winner . . . the Team Blue Crew!

Grumpy Judge: Great . . . . Can I go home now?

THE END

Team Blue's Rally 2: **The Script**

Zeus onstage alone.

Zeus: Oh no, it's time for the big game already! I can't believe I have to do this by myself.

Jupiter and Bella enter.

Jupiter: Ready for the big game there, Zeussy?

Zeus: Um . . . yes, I am . . . err . . . who are you?

Jupiter: The name's Jupiter.

Zeus: I guess you're here to help cheer on Team Blue?

Jupiter: No way! I'm here to make sure Red wins!

Bella: RED IS GOOD! RED'S THE BEST! BETTER THAN A YELLOW VEST! GOOOO, RED!

Zeus: But, um . . . I'm supposed to be the moose mascot! I thought Team Red's mascot was an alien!

Jupiter: Antenna was LAST year's mascot!

Bella: LAST YEAR'S OUT! THIS YEAR'S IN!

Jeff the referee and both teams enter.

Jeff: All right, everyone ready for some dodgeball?

Jupiter: Never been more ready, Jeff! EVERYONE, LEMME HEAR YA SAY MOOOSE!

Team Red: MOOOSE!

Zeus: Wait, um . . . hey . . . that's MY line!

Jupiter: No, I'm pretty sure it's MINE there, Zeussy!

Jeff: Whoa, whoa, whoa! Time out! Be a good sport! Cheers are for everyone!

Scoreboard breaks.

Jeff: Oh, great, now the scoreboard's broken!

Bella: OOPS OOPS GOES THE CLOCK! USED TO TICK BUT NOW IT TOCKS!

Zeus: Maybe we could just play for fun instead?

Jupiter: No way! You want this trophy back? You'll have to earn it! This is TEAM RED'S time to shine!

Bella: HE'S GONNA SHINE THE CLOCK!

Jupiter: Not THAT kind of shine, Bella.

Zeus: You know what?! I've had enough of this! YOU'RE NOT THE ONLY MOOSE IN TOWN! I'm gonna show you who the original moose is! ARE YOU READY, TEAM BLUE?!

Team Blue: YES!!!

Zeus: Then let's bring this trophy BACK HOME!

Team Blue: GO, TEAM BLUE!

Jupiter: We'll see who this trophy belongs to . . .

Jeff: Game on!

Whistle blows and the game begins.

THE END

Team Blue vs Team Red: The Script

Jeff: Welcome to the final match of the Dodgeball Championship!

Zeus: All right, here we go. Don't get nervous. Don't get nervous.

Tate: Arr! Don't worry, Zeus, we're ready for this. Chin up, sailor!

Zeus: I'll try.

Jeff: In this corner we have those marvelous mascots, the BLUE TEAM! And in this corner, we have the defending champs, the RED TEAM!

Scarlet: Well, this should be easy, right, Eric?

Eric: . . .

Scarlet: Ha-ha! Good one!

Jeff: All right, guys, I want a nice, friendly game. I mean it.

Scarlet: You got it, ref. A nice, SHORT, friendly game.

Tate: Hey! I heard that!

Jeff: All right, here we go. GAME ON!

Scarlet: Ready or not, here comes my super ultra mega power ball!

Scarlet throws a dodgeball.

Zeus: Yikes! That almost took my antlers off!

Tate: Look out, Zeus!

Eric throws a dodgeball and misses.

Tate: HA! Is that all you got?

Eric: . . .

Eric throws a dodgeball, and pegs Tate!

Tate: Oh no! I'm down! I'm down!

Scarlet: Ha ha ha! More like Tate the SUNKEN Migrator!

Jeff: TWEET! Clean hit! Tate is out!

Eric: . . .

Zeus: Oh no! I'm all alone! I can't do this!

Scarlet: All right, just one more power ball, and this game is OVER!

Jeff: TWEET! Foul! Too many shoes on the court!

Zeus: Wait, what?

Jeff: Someone has to take off his or her shoes. I mean it!

Scarlet: Fine, I'll take off my shoes.

Jeff: Game on!

Scarlet: All right, Zeus, any last words before you're out?

Zeus: Umm . . . How about "yikes"!

Jeff: TWEET! Foul! No saying "yikes" on the court!

Scarlet: What? That's just silly!

Zeus: Umm, sorry? I won't do it again . . .

Jeff: Game on!

Scarlet: As I was saying, here comes my most powerful dodgeball!

Jeff: TWEET! Foul!

Scarlet: Now what?!

Jeff: Your name is too long. You must shorten it.

Scarlet: Okay, this is getting crazy! I'm just going to throw the ball.

Scarlet throws a dodgeball.

Zeus: Gadzooks!

Dodgeball misses Zeus, rebounds back.

Scarlet: Look out! Runaway dodgeball!

Eric: ! ! !

Dodgeball misses Team Red, rebounds, and hits Jeff!

Jeff: TWEET! Clean hit! The ref is out!

Zeus: But wait . . . YOU'RE the ref!

Scarlet: Yeah, I didn't mean to hit you.

Jeff: Doesn't matter. Rules are rules. TWEET! Game on!!

Scarlet: All right, then. Let's finish this, Blue Team!

Zeus: You're on!

They finish the game. It's up to you to decide who wins!

Tate: And the winner is . . .

Everyone: RED TEAM!

Everyone: BLUE TEAM!

Everyone: IT'S A TIE!

THE END

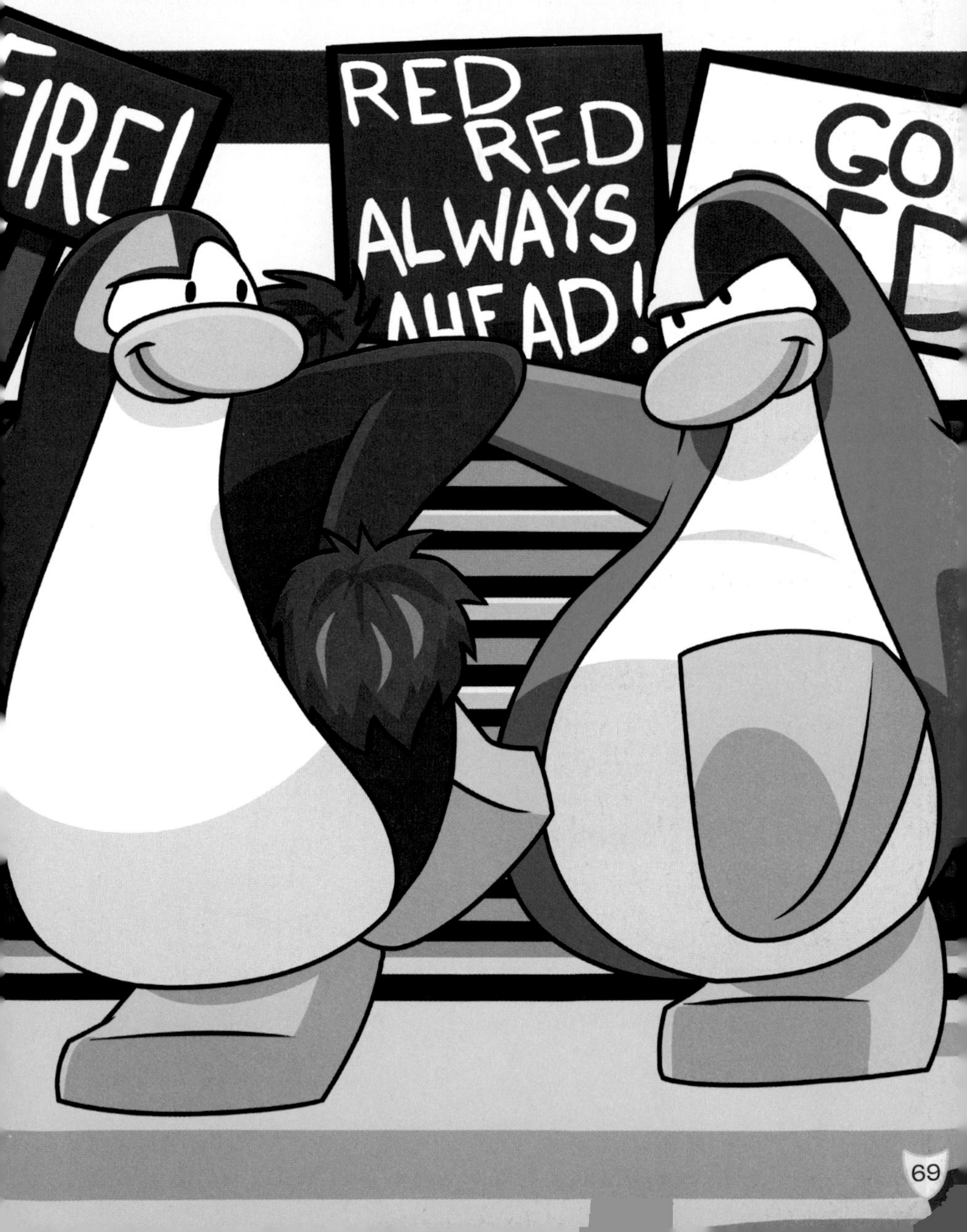
RED
RED
ALWAYS
GO

Show your team spirit with a cheer-filled production of *Team Rally*!

Costume Creator

Zeus and Jupiter: Wear a blue shirt for Zeus and a red one for Jupiter. Make moose antlers out of construction paper and attach to a headband.

Peppy: Paint a paper plate orange. When dry, glue on feathers and draw on a beak. Make sure to cut out holes for the eyes. Glue on a Popsicle stick and hold over your face to look like Peppy.

Tate: Go for a pirate look. Tie a bandana around your head and put on an eye patch. If you don't have a patch, cut one out of paper. Cut small holes on each side. Tie yarn or elastic through the slits to hold the patch on your head.

Make a Scene

All you need is a wide-open space. For *Team Blue's Rally Debut*, a table and three chairs for the judges are all the extras you'll need. For *Team Blue's Rally 2* and *Team Blue vs Team Red*, a couple of balls will help set the scene for the dodgeball game.

The Twelfth Fish

As Court Jester, I always like to have fun, but there was one question that was troubling me: To fish or not to fish? The Countess, Bard, and I answered it when we took to the seas to cast our lines. We managed to catch a fish that was quite fit for the dish!

The Characters

Court Jester
I'm so funny, I can even make a fish laugh!

Countess
This fair maiden finds that fishing is such sweet comfort.

The Bard
Don't let the fancy collar fool you. The Bard knows his way around a fishing boat.

Fish
Do my ears deceive me, or is my dinner talking to me?

The Story

What else would a penguin want to do on a bright and sunny day but fish? We all set out on the ocean waves with our fishing poles, trading prose all the while. Our trip was a success. We caught the biggest yellow fish I've ever seen!

Since this set has no Switchbox, try clicking on the clouds, sun, and moon to see what happens.

When you read the script for *The Twelfth Fish*, you might notice that the characters have a funny way of talking. That's because *The Twelfth Fish* is an ode to William Shakespeare, one of the most famous writers to have ever lived. Shakespeare, who lived almost 400 years ago, wrote lots and lots of plays, and he wrote in an old English style—which is why the words sound so unusual. One of his plays is called *The Twelfth Night*. Sound familiar?

STAGE SECRETS

The Twelfth Fish: The Script

Countess: The Iceberg's a stage and we are penguins!

Jester: A stage where every penguin plays a part.

Bard: Fair maiden, shall we go and catch some fish?

Jester: To fish or not to fish, that is the question!

Countess: Good plan! Fishing is such sweet comfort.

Bard: Now is the winter of our fishing trip.

Jester: As good luck would have it!

Bard: The first thing we do, let's catch all the fish.

Fish: BLUB BLUB!

Jester: O fishing line, fishing line! Wherefore art thou doing fine?

Fish: BLUBBETH!

Countess: What fish through yonder ocean swim?

Fish: DOUBLE, DOUBLE, BLUB AND BUBBLE!

Bard: But hark! What fish through yonder water peeks?

Jester: A fish! A fish! My puffle for a fish!

Fish: AY, THERE'S THE BLUB!

Countess: Something fishy this way comes.

Jester: With my empty tummy my eye doth feast.

Bard: Now please get me a dish fit for the fish!

Fish: BUT NEVER DOUBT I BLUB!

Countess: Get thee to a fishery!

Jester: To dine, perchance to eat!

Bard: If fish be the food of life, waddle on!

The End

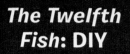

Perform this ode to fish by making a few simple props and costumes.

Costume Creator

Court Jester: Cut a strip of paper long enough to go around your head and decorate it. Cut out long triangles from different colored paper. Tape or glue the triangles to the inside of the cardboard crown. Staple the cardboard ends together before placing on your head. Then fold down the triangles.

Countess: Roll a piece of paper into a cone shape and tape at the end. Then decorate and attach a ribbon to the point of the hat. Wear a pretty dress.

Bard: Wear a white shirt with a vest, shorts, and white socks. A beret will complete the look.

Fish: Dress all in yellow. Make a fish mask out of a paper plate and a Popsicle stick.

Make a Scene

Houseplants or fake flowers can serve as the garden. A blue sheet, tablecloth, or towel can be used for the ocean. A big box turned upside down can make a great boat. So can a few chairs pushed together. Use sticks for fishing poles.

Penguin Playwrights

You don't have to stick to the script when you are putting on a show at The Stage. Get creative! Make up your own lines, write your own play, or mix up characters, costumes, and scripts from past plays to come up with your own unique production!

How to Write Your Own Play

There's a lot more that goes into a play than acting, directing, and set production. First, someone needs to write the play! If you'd like to become a penguin playwright, here are a few things to think about before you get started:

Setting: Where do you want your play to take place: at the Iceberg, an amusement park, a concert, or somewhere else?

Characters: Who is your play about? What do your characters look like? What are they like?

Plot: What happens in your play? Are your characters having an adventure? Is it a slapstick comedy? It's up to you!

Having a hard time coming up with ideas? Try combining plays that are already on the site to make an entirely new one. What if Zeus, Peppy, and Tate entered the Great Pyramid to search for the golden puffle? Or if Shadow Guy and Gamma Gal were the ones to cheer on the Blue Team at the dodgeball game? Imagine the cave penguins from *The Penguins That Time Forgot* setting out on a fishing trip. Or Twee as the captain of the *SS Astro-Barrier*. You can make it happen!

Or, pick a random combination of your favorite things to make up a new play. You could write a play about a chef who lost his top secret pizza recipe. Or a dancer who is trying to become the top scorer at the Night Club's Dance Contest. What would happen if a ninja ended up in a haunted house with a ghost? You could write about any of these things or use your imagination to create your own original play.

Once you've written your masterpiece, perform it! Head over to The Stage and use the tips on page 6 to put on your show. Or put your play on anywhere using the DIY tips throughout this book.

Curtain Call

Don't be sad when the applause is finished and the audience has gone home. You can start working on a new production right away. Remember to always be on the lookout for new plays at The Stage. Before you know it, you'll be taking bows again!